This Book is dedicated to Ashley & Lia.

DOODIE & THE CHOCOLATE

Written By Franco Tingle

Illustrated by Shawn Gaines

I hope you enjoy. Best wishes!!!

I hope you enjoy. best wishes !!!

Doodie is a wonderful 4-year-old girl who's lots of fun. No, her real name is not Doodie, silly. Doodie is the nickname that she gave herself. She likes to be called Doodie because she knows it makes her different, and Doodie loves being different!!

Doodie is also very independent. She does not have any sisters or brothers to play with so she plays make-believe and has lots of fun all by herself.

Doodie lives with her Mommy, Daddy, and Otis. Otis is Doodie's black pug. Doodie loves her Otis!!! She feeds Otis and lets him outside to use the bathroom before school.

Otis loves to cuddle with Doodie, which brings a big smile to her face. She treats Otis like a baby even though Otis is older than she is. Otis always sniffs Doodie because she eats and smells like chocolate.

One night, Doodie's Daddy gave her a piece of chocolate while her Mommy was fixing dinner. She ate the chocolate in one bite.

It was so delicious!!!

Her Daddy told her she could not have any more chocolate until after she had eaten all her dinner. She didn't like it that her Daddy wouldn't let her have more chocolate. She still agreed not to eat any more chocolate until after dinner even though it was calling her…. Doodie…. Doodie.

Doodie's Mommy didn't hear Doodie's Daddy tell her that she couldn't have more chocolate. Doodie knew she could not have any more chocolate until after dinner, but she just had to have more!!! She asked her Mommy for a piece of chocolate using her sweetest voice. How could her Mommy tell her little angel no?

Doodie's Mommy gave her a piece of chocolate that was even bigger than the piece her Daddy had given her. She ate the chocolate.

YUMMMY!!

Doodie's Mommy finished cooking dinner. She and her parents sat down at the table to eat. Her Mommy had cooked macaroni and cheese and barbeque chicken. This was Doodie's favorite dinner!! She even gave Doodie fruit punch to drink, which is her favorite drink.

Mommy and Daddy began to eat, but Doodie did not take even one bite of her food. Doodie had a tummy ache from the chocolate she had eaten. She was fine until she ate that second piece. She knew she was wrong for asking her mother for a second piece of chocolate.
She had disobeyed her Daddy.

Doodie decided that she would tell her Mommy she was not hungry if her Mommy asked her what was wrong. Sure enough, Doodie's Mommy asked, "What's wrong, baby? You haven't touched your food." Her Mommy knew something was wrong because she had cooked Doodie's favorite dinner. Doodie said, "I'm not really that hungry, Mommy."

Her Mommy found that hard to believe. Doodie's Mommy thought she had not eaten since lunch except for the piece of chocolate she had given Doodie.

Doodie's Mommy said, "What's wrong, baby? I want you to tell me the truth." Doodie said, "I have a tummy ache from the chocolate I ate." Her stomach was feeling very bad. Her Mommy said, "Poor baby, I only gave you one piece."

Doodie's Daddy asked her Mommy, "Why did you give her a piece of chocolate?" Doodie started to cry as she thought about how she had disobeyed her Daddy.

Doodie's Mommy told her Daddy that she had given her a piece of chocolate because her little angel had asked in such the sweetest voice. Her Daddy told her Mommy that he had already given Doodie a piece of chocolate, and she was not supposed to eat any more chocolate until after she had eaten all her dinner.

Doodie's Mommy asked her if this were true. Doodie began to cry and in her saddest voice said, "Yes." Her Mommy and Daddy told her to stop crying. They told her that disobeying her parents was not nice. They told her that she should always be honest even when she does something wrong. Doodie told them that she was sorry.

She was really sorry that she had disobeyed her Daddy. Her Mommy gave her three crackers and a small cup of ginger ale to settle her stomach, and then told her to go upstairs to her room and get ready for bed.

Doodie was feeling better by bedtime, but she was so sad thinking that her Daddy was disappointed in her that she started to cry.

Her Daddy overheard her crying and went into the bedroom. "What's wrong?" asked her Daddy.

Doodie sobbed, "I'm sorry I ate another piece of chocolate."

Her Daddy kissed her cheek and wiped away her tears. He told her to do what her parents say, no matter which parent tells her to do something. He gave Doodie a big hug and another kiss. Doodie was smiling from ear to ear because she loves her Daddy so much!!! They did their secret handshake, and Doodie fell fast asleep.

The next day Doodie woke up feeling great. Her Mommy only had to tell her once to brush her teeth. Doodie even got dressed without having to be told to do so more than twice. She ate breakfast and let Otis out to use the bathroom. She went to school after feeding Otis.

Doodie's Daddy picked her up from school in the afternoon and they drove home. She asked her Daddy for some chocolate and he said not until after dinner. Doodie was fine with that because she knew super girls listen to their parents. Her Mommy walked into the house and asked, "Doodie, do you want a piece of chocolate?" Doodie said, "No thanks, I already asked Daddy, and he said I can't have any until after dinner."

THE
END

Made in the USA
Monee, IL
12 December 2020